W9-BKB-307

Corduroy
A Pocket for Corduroy

Don Freeman

Corduroy

Copyright © Don Freeman, 1968

A Pocket for Corduroy

Copyright © Don Freeman, 1978

All rights reserved. No part of this book may be used or
reproduced in any manner whatsoever without the written permission
of Penguin Putnam Inc., 375 Hudson Street, New York, N.Y. 10014.

This edition published by Borders Group, Inc.,
by arrangement with The Viking Press, a member of Penguin Putnam Books for Young Readers.

Printed and Bound in Mexico

ISBN 0-681-88921-7

02 M 9 8 7 6 5 4

CORDUROY

Story and Pictures by Don Freeman

THE VIKING PRESS / NEW YORK

To Sally Elizabeth Kildow
and Patrick Steven Duff Kildow,
who know how a bear feels about buttons

A bear's share of the author's royalties from the sale of *Corduroy* goes to the *Don and Lydia Freeman Research Fund* to support psychological research concerning children afflicted with cancer.

Corduroy is a bear who once lived in the toy department of a big store. Day after day he waited with all the other animals and dolls for somebody to come along and take him home.

The store was always filled with shoppers buying all sorts of things, but no one ever seemed to want a small bear in green overalls.

Then one morning a little girl stopped and looked straight into Corduroy's bright eyes.

"Oh, Mommy!" she said. "Look! There's the very bear I've always wanted."

"Not today, dear." Her mother sighed. "I've spent too much already. Besides, he doesn't look new. He's lost the button to one of his shoulder straps."

Corduroy watched them sadly as they walked away.

"I didn't know I'd lost a button," he said to himself. "Tonight I'll go and see if I can find it."

Late that evening, when all the shoppers had gone and the doors were shut and locked, Corduroy climbed carefully down from his

shelf and began searching everywhere on the floor for his lost
button.

Suddenly he felt the floor moving under him! Quite by accident he had stepped onto an escalator—and up he went!

"Could this be a mountain?" he wondered. "I think I've always wanted to climb a mountain."

He stepped off the escalator as it reached the next floor, and there, before his eyes, was a most amazing sight—

tables and chairs and lamps and sofas, and rows and rows of beds.
"This must be a palace!" Corduroy gasped. "I guess I've always
wanted to live in a palace."

He wandered around admiring the furniture.
"This must be a bed," he said. "I've always wanted to sleep in a bed." And up he crawled onto a large, thick mattress.

All at once he saw something small and round.
"Why, here's my button!" he cried. And he tried to pick it up. But,
like all the other buttons on the mattress, it was tied down tight.

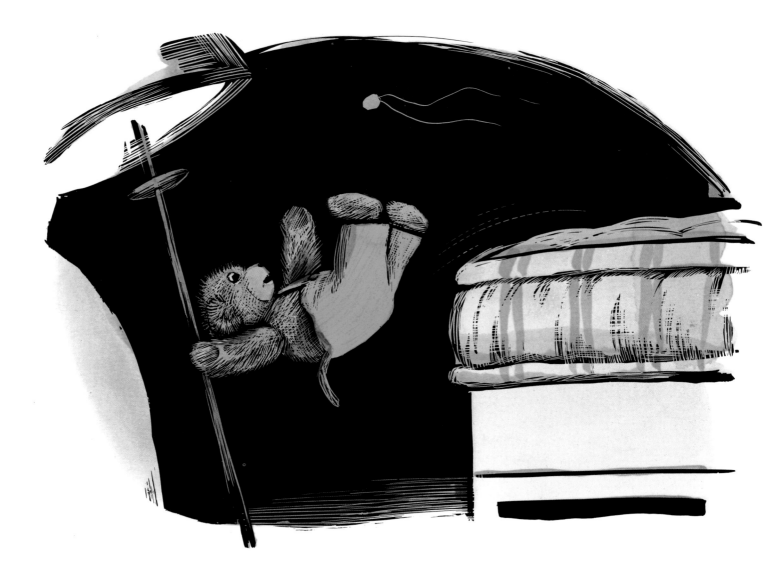

He yanked and pulled with both paws until POP! Off came the button—and off the mattress Corduroy toppled,

bang into a tall floor lamp. Over it fell with a crash!

Corduroy didn't know it, but there was someone else awake in the store. The night watchman was going his rounds on the floor above. When he heard the crash he came dashing down the escalator.

"Now who in the world did that!" he exclaimed. "Somebody must be hiding around here!"

He flashed his light under and over sofas and beds until he came to the biggest bed of all. And there he saw two fuzzy brown ears sticking up from under the cover.

"Hello!" he said. "How did *you* get upstairs?"

The watchman tucked Corduroy under his arm and carried him down the escalator

and set him on the shelf in the toy department with the other
animals and dolls.

Corduroy was just waking up when the first customers came into the store in the morning. And there, looking at him with a wide, warm smile, was the same little girl he'd seen only the day before.

"I'm Lisa," she said, "and you're going to be my very own bear. Last night I counted what I've saved in my piggy bank and my mother said I could bring you home."

"Shall I put him in a box for you?" the saleslady asked.

"Oh, no thank you," Lisa answered. And she carried Corduroy home in her arms.

She ran all the way up four flights of stairs, into her family's apartment, and straight to her own room.

Corduroy blinked. There was a chair and a chest of drawers, and alongside a girl-size bed stood a little bed just the right size for him. The room was small, nothing like that enormous palace in the department store.

"This must be home," he said. "I *know* I've always wanted a home!"

Lisa sat down with Corduroy on her lap and began to sew a button
on his overalls.

"I like you the way you are," she said, "but you'll be more
comfortable with your shoulder strap fastened."

"You must be a friend," said Corduroy. "I've always wanted a friend."

"Me too!" said Lisa, and gave him a big hug.

A POCKET FOR CORDUROY

story and pictures by DON FREEMAN

To Takako Nishinoya,

who knows how a bear feels about pockets

A bear's share of the author's royalties from the sale of *A Pocket For Corduroy* goes to the *Don and Lydia Freeman Research Fund* to support psychological research concerning children afflicted with cancer.

Late one summer afternoon Lisa and her mother took their laundry to the laundromat.

As always on such trips Lisa carried along her toy bear, Corduroy.

The laundromat was a very busy place at this hour.

"Now, Corduroy, you sit right here and wait for me," Lisa said. "I'm going to help with our wash."

Corduroy waited patiently. Then he suddenly perked up his ears.

Lisa's mother was saying, "Be sure to take everything out of your pockets, Lisa dear. You don't want your precious things to get all wet and soapy."

"Pockets?" said Corduroy to himself. "I don't have a pocket!"

He slid off the chair. "I must go find something to make a pocket out of," he said, and he began to look around.

First he came to a pile of fancy towels and washcloths, but nothing was the right size or color.

Then he saw a huge stack of colorful clothes in a laundry bag. "There ought to be something in there to make a pocket out of," he said.

Without hesitating, he climbed inside the bag, which was filled with pieces of wet laundry. The dampness didn't bother Corduroy in the least. "This must be a cave," he said, sighing happily. "I've always wanted to live in a dark, cool cave."

When the time came for Lisa to fetch her bear, he was gone.

"Oh, Mommy!" she exclaimed. "Corduroy isn't here where I left him!"

"I'm sorry, honey," said her mother, "but the laundromat will be closing soon and we must be getting home."

Lisa was reluctant to leave without Corduroy, but her mother insisted. "You can come back tomorrow," she said. "I'm sure he will still be here."

As they left, a young man wearing an artist's beret was taking his
wet laundry out of a bag—the very bag Corduroy had discovered!

Before he knew it, Corduroy was being tossed, together with all the
sheets, shirts, shorts, and slacks . . .

inside the dryer.

But just as the artist was shutting the glass door, Corduroy tumbled out onto the floor.

"How in thunder did that bear ever get mixed up with all my things?" the artist wondered.

Poor Corduroy was damp all over.

"The least I can do for him is give his overalls a good drying," said the man thoughtfully. He unbuttoned Corduroy's shoulder straps and put his overalls in the dryer.

Corduroy grew dizzy as he watched the clothes spinning around, but the artist became inspired. "This would make a wonderful painting!" he said as he took a sketch pad out of his pocket and began drawing the swirling colors. "I can hardly wait to get back to my studio."

Finally the dryer stopped whirling and the man gathered up the clothes. Then he helped Corduroy put on his warm, dry overalls.

All at once the manager of the laundromat called, "Closing time! Everybody out!"

Corduroy was gently placed on top of a washing machine.

"I wonder who that bear belongs to," said the artist as he was leaving.

"Seems to me he should have his name someplace. He's too fine a fellow to be lost."

As soon as the lights were turned off, Corduroy began his search again. He was surprised to see something white glowing in the dark. "Maybe it's snow!" he said excitedly. "I've always wanted to play in the snow."

He accidentally tipped over the open-lidded box, and suddenly he was covered with soft, slippery soap flakes.

Gradually Corduroy began to slip and slide....

"Oh, what fun!" he said with a smile. "I've always wanted to ski down a steep mountainside."

He landed paws first in an empty laundry basket.

"This must be a cage," he said, peeking through the bars. "I've *never* wanted to live inside a cage like a bear in the zoo!"

But by now Corduroy felt drowsy, and soon he nodded off to sleep.

Next morning when the manager came to open the door of the laundromat, there was Lisa waiting.

"I left something here yesterday," she explained. "May I look around?"

"Certainly," said the manager. "My customers are always leaving things."

Lisa was searching under the chairs and in back of the washing machines when she heard the manager call her. "Is this what you're looking for, señorita?"

"Yes, yes! He's my best friend!" shouted Lisa as she came running. She reached in and picked Corduroy out of the basket. "So this is where you've been, you little rascal!" she said. "It's time I took you home!"

Lisa thanked the manager and ran out the door and down the street, holding Corduroy tightly in her arms. "I thought I told you to wait for me," she said. "Why did you wander away?"

"I went looking for a pocket," Corduroy said.

"Oh, Corduroy! Why didn't you tell me you wanted a pocket?" asked Lisa, giving him an affectionate squeeze.

That very morning Lisa sewed a pocket on Corduroy's overalls. "And here is a card I've made with your name on it for you to keep tucked inside," she said.

"I've always wanted a purple pocket with my name tucked inside," said Corduroy as he and Lisa nuzzled noses.